James and the Red Balloon
AND OTHER THOMAS THE TANK ENGINE STORIES

Random House 🏠 **New York**

A Random House PICTUREBACK® Book

Photographs by David Mitton, Terry Palone, and Terry Permane for Britt Allcroft's
production of *Thomas the Tank Engine and Friends*

Thomas the Tank Engine & Friends®

A BRITT ALLCROFT COMPANY PRODUCTION
Based on The Railway Series by The Reverend W Awdry.
© 2004 Gullane (Thomas) Limited

A HIT Entertainment Company
All rights reserved under International and Pan-American Copyright Conventions.
Published in the United States by Random House Children's Books, a division of Random House, Inc., New York,
and simultaneously in Canada by Random House of Canada Limited, Toronto.

www.randomhouse.com/kids/thomas   www.thomasthetankengine.com

Library of Congress Control Number: 2003005743

ISBN 0-375-82753-6 Printed in the United States of America First Edition 10 9 8

• James and the Red Balloon •

It is summer holiday time on the Island of Sodor. Vacationers come from far and wide to enjoy the be[...]f the island. It is the busiest time of the year for Sir Topham H[...]es ngines.

Thomas was excited. Sir Topha[...] h att had sent him to pick up a special to deliver to Dryaw Airfiel[...]

"What have you got there?" tooted Percy.

"A balloon," replied Thomas.

"A party balloon?" asked Percy excitedly.

"No," said Thomas. "This is a very special balloon." And he chuffed away.

Soon Thomas arrived at the airfield. And hot air was puffed into the balloon.

"What is that?" huffed Jam

"A hot-air balloon," said T omas. "It will take vacationers on rides around the island!"

"Taking vacationers on rides around the island is *our* job," wheeshed James jealously. Then, as if by magic, the hot-air balloon rose silently up into the sky.

"What if the hot-air balloon takes our passengers away?" chuffed James. "What will happen to us then?"

This made Thomas worry. Suddenly he wasn't so excited about the balloon. The balloon could be seen by everyone on the Island of Sodor. Duck gazed at it for so long, he ran into the back of Stepney.

"Why, it's a floating basket with folks in it," said Donald.

"Whatever will they dream up next?" said Douglas.

James and Thomas were waiting at the level crossing. They were still worried about the hot-air balloon. "If it takes our passengers away," chuffed Thomas, "there'll be no use for us engines."

"Passengers should travel on trains!" huffed James. "Not in silly balloons."

Then something big and round and red drifted straight towards them.

"We're out of hot air!" shouted a voice.

"ARRRRGGGGGGGHHHHHHH!" cried James. "What's happening?"

Crash! Bang! Wallop! went the balloon, and landed right on top of James. He was so scared, he let out a huge burst of steam, which blew the balloon up again.

The balloon rose into the air once more.

"Well done, James!" called his driver. "Your hot air did the trick."

"Oh, no, James!" cried Thomas. "You saved the hot-air balloon!"

"I didn't mean to!" groaned James. "Now it's *sure* to take our passengers."

Wherever James went, he could see the balloon carrying vacationers across the island. He felt *he* should be taking those passengers. "Rails are better than hot air any day."

James arrived back at the station. There were lots of people on the platform.

Sir Topham Hatt was waiting, too. "Well done, James!"

"But now the passengers will ride in the hot-air balloon."

Sir Topham Hatt laughed.

"You're right, James," he said. "But they will need a ride home—in a train!"

James was delighted.

pham Hatt was right. The engines were busier
ver taking vacationers to and from the airfield.
henever James sees the red balloon, he whistles and
oots. And sometimes, when he's asleep at night, James
dreams he can fly, too . . .

. . . just like the red balloon!

The engines on Sir Topham Hatt's ra
Brendam Docks. There's always lots of
keep them busy. And they enjoy seeing
arrivals onto the Island of Sodor.

An exciting new arrival was an eng
the Crane was unloading. It was heavy.
makes my chain ache," groaned Cranky

"This is Harvey the Crane Engine," Sir Topham Hatt said proudly. The other engines thought Harvey looked strange. Harvey was happy to be on the ground. He didn't like dangling from Cranky's arm at all.

"These gentlemen are the Railway Board," Sir Topham Hatt said. "Tomorrow Harvey will give them a demonstration. If it goes well, he will join the railway."

"What's a dimmer station?"

"Demonstration," said Thomas. "It's when you show off what you can do."

"Like when Thomas and I have a race," said Bertie. *Vrrroooom! Vrrroooom!*

That evening, Thomas had just returned from a hard day's work. He saw Harvey parked near the sheds. Harvey could hear the other engines talking about him. This made him sad.

"Harvey's different," said Henry.

"He doesn't even *look* like an engine," said Edward.

"Surely Sir Topham Hatt won't let him pull coaches," sniffed Gordon.

"He's just Cranky on wheels," said James.

"He's not taking *my* mail," said Percy.

Thomas felt sorry for Harvey. "Don't worry. Sometimes it takes time to make new friends!"

But Harvey wasn't sure he wanted to stay where no one wanted him.

The next morning, Sir Topham Hatt sent the engines off to a useful day's work. "Maybe my coming here wasn't such a good idea, Sir," Harvey chuffed sadly.

"Nonsense!" said Sir Topham Hatt.

"But the engines don't like me. I'm too different."

"Different is what makes you special." And that made Harvey feel better.

Out on the branch line, Percy was having trouble with the trucks. "Faster we go. Faster we go. Pull him along. Don't let him slow!"

"*Heelllp!*" cried Percy. His driver applied the brakes . . .

. . . but it was too late. He went off the rails at Bulgy's Bridge. Luckily, no one was hurt.

Bertie arrived and was pleased Percy was all right. But he was also very cross. "You've blocked the road!" Bertie snapped. He was worried he wouldn't get the gentlemen of the Railway Board to the demonstration on time.

When Sir Topham Hatt heard the news, he went
straight to Harvey. "I need you to rescue one of my
engines!"

"I'll do my best, Sir!" Harvey said bravely. And he set
off immediately.

Harvey soon arrived and went to work. In no time,
Percy was back on the tracks. The gentlemen of the
Railway Board were very impressed.

"That was the best demonstration of all! The gentlemen of the Railway Board have decided you shall join the railway."

"Oh, thank you, Sir," said Harvey proudly.

That night, Harvey heard the engines talking again. This time it was different. "Well done, Harvey," said Gordon.

"Very useful," said James.

"You can take my mail," said Percy.

"You see," said Thomas. "Different can be good!"

All the engines agreed. "Welcome to the Sodor Railway," they called.

Harvey smiled happily.

• Thomas the Jet Engine •

Gordon is a very proud steam engine. He's the fastest engine on the Island of Sodor. He loves speeding along his line with the wind blowing across his funnel.

"You've broken the record again," said his driver.

"I'm the fastest," boasted Gordon.

But not all the engines were impressed. "Speed isn't everything," said James smugly.

"But being reliable and useful is," said Thomas.

"You slow engines will never understand," snorted Gordon. "Because you'll never go as fast as me!"

Sir Topham Hatt arrived with news of a special for Thomas. "I want you to collect a jet engine and take it to the airfield."

"What's a jet engine?" asked Percy.

"A jet engine goes forward by pushing hot air out of its back," Sir Topham Hatt explained.

"Just like when you blow up a balloon and let it go," added Thomas. "It's very fast."

Thomas likes making special deliveries for Sir Topham Hatt. It makes him feel special. But secretly he wished he could go as fast as Gordon. Just once.

Thomas arrived at the docks excited to see the jet engine. It was shiny and modern, and Thomas had never seen anything like it. He couldn't wait to start his journey. But Cranky was taking his time. "Hurry up," huffed Thomas. "This is a *special* special."

Cranky did not like being told what to do. Especially by an engine. He became so cranky that he was careless with his hook.

His hook knocked the switch. And the switch started the jet engine. And the engine began to whine. The whine got louder and louder . . . and louder . . . and louder . . .

"Uh-oh," said Cranky. Before he could say anything else, the jet engine was rocketing Thomas up the track!

"OHHHHHH!" said Thomas.

The driver tried to put on the brakes. But Thomas couldn't stop.

"OHHHHH, BOYYY!"

The stationmaster called ahead . . .

"Clear the lines! It's a runaway train!"

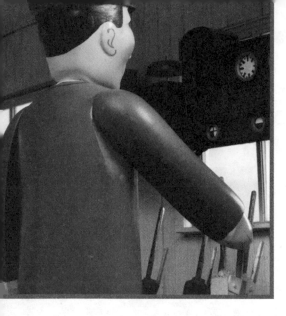

Signals were changed and points were switched. Thomas had never been so excited. Thomas flew by James . . . and rocketed past Henry . . . and raced by Percy. They were amazed.

Bertie was excited when he saw Thomas flying down the track. "Want a race, Thomas?" beeped Bertie. "Uh . . . never mind." No one had ever seen an engine go so fast!

Gordon had no idea that Thomas was racing along the main line. "I am the fastest!" said Gordon proudly.

"Hi, Gordon! . . . Bye, Gordon!"

Gordon could not believe what he had seen.

At last the jet engine ran out of fuel and Thomas was back under his own power. He steamed gently back into Knapford Station.

"Sorry for overtaking you back there, Gordon!" teased Thomas.

"Overtake me? I didn't notice," Gordon huffed.

"You didn't notice the fastest engine on the Island of Sodor?" said Henry.

"Yes. I am the fastest!" puffed Thomas.

Percy felt a little sorry for Gordon. "Gordon doesn't have to go as fast as a jet engine. He's a steam engine."

"But he's *still* full of hot air!" whistled James.

And Gordon wheeshed away.

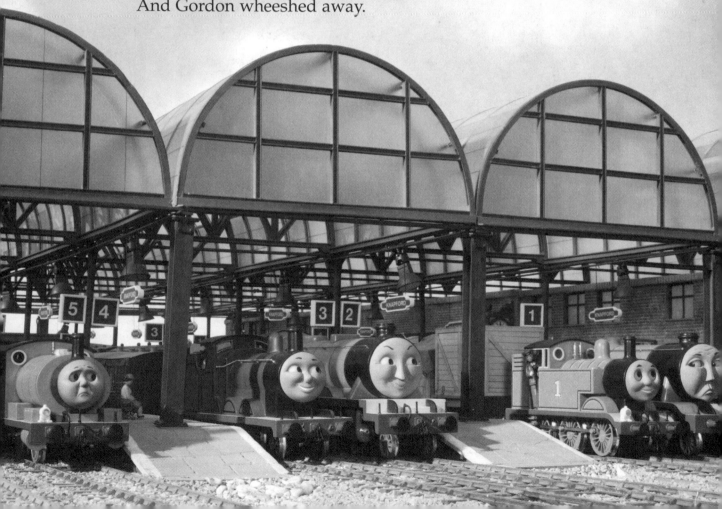